René GOSCINNY and Albert UDERZO

present

THE TWELVE TASKS OF
ASTERIX

based on the cartoon film created by

STUDIO IDEFIX

HODDER DARGAUD

LONDON SYDNEY AUCKLAND

ASTERIX IN OTHER COUNTRIES

Australia	Hodder Dargaud, 2 Apollo Place, Lane Cove, New South Wales 2066
Austria	Delta Verlag, Postfach 1215, 7 Stuttgart 1, G.F.R.
Belgium	Dargaud Bénélux, 3 rue Kindermans, 1050 Brussels
Brazil	Cedibra, rua Filomena Nunes 162, Rio de Janeiro
Canada	Dargaud Canada, 307 Benjamin-Hudon, St. Laurent, Montreal P.Q. H4N1J1
Denmark	Gutenberghus Bladene, Vognmagergade 11, 1148 Copenhagen K
Finland	Sanoma Osakeyhtio, Ludviginkatu 2—10, 00130 Helsinki 13
France	Regional Editions
	(Langue d'Oc) Société Toulousaine du Livre, Avenue de Larrieu, 31094 Toulouse
German Federal Republic	Delta Verlag, Postfach 1215, 7 Stuttgart 1, G.F.R.
Greece	Anglo-Hellenic Agency, Kriezotou 3, Syntagma, Athens 134, Greece
Holland	Dargaud Bénélux, 3 rue Kindermans, 1050 Brussels, Belgium
	(Distribution) Oberon, Ceylonpoort 5—25, Haarlem, Holland
Hong Kong	Hodder Dargaud, c/o United Publishers Service Private Ltd, Stanhope House, 734 King's Road
Iceland	Fjolvi HF, Njorvasund 15a, Reykjavik
Indonesia	Pt Sinar Kasih, Tromolpos 260, Jakarta
Israel	Dahlia Pelled Publishers, P.O. Box 33325, Tel Aviv
Italy	Arnoldo Mondadori Editore, 1 Via Belvedere, 37131 Verona
Latin America	Grijalbo-Dargaud S.A., Deu y Mata 98—102, Barcelona 29
New Zealand	Hodder Dargaud, P.O. Box 3858, Auckland 1
Norway	A/S Hjemmet (Gutenburghus Group), Kristian den 4des Gate 13, Oslo 1
Portugal	Meriberica, rua D. Filipa de Vilherna 4—5°, Lisbon 1
Roman Empire	*(Latin)* Delta Verlag, Postfach 1215, 7 Stuttgart 1, G.F.R.
South Africa	*(English)* Hodder Dargaud, P.O. Box 32213, Braamfontein Centre, Braamfontein 2017 Johannesburg
Spain	Grijalbo-Dargaud S.A., Deu y Mata 98—102, Barcelona 29
Sweden	Hemmets Journal Forlag (Gutenburghes Group), Fack, 200 22 Malmo
Switzerland	Interpress Dargaud, En Budron B, 1052 Le Mont/Lausanne
Turkey	Kervan Kitabcilik, Serefendi Sokagi 31, Cagaloglu-Istanbul
Wales	*(Welsh)* Gwasg Y Dref Wen, 28 Church Road, Yr Eglwys Newydd, Cardiff CF4 2EA
Yugoslavia	Nip Forum, Vojvode Misica 1—3, 2100 Novi Sad

ISBN 0 340 22752 4 (cased edition)
ISBN 0 340 27647 9 (paperbound edition)

Copyright © 1976 Dargaud Editeur
English language text copyright © 1976 Hodder & Stoughton Ltd

First published in Great Britain 1978 (cased)

First published in Great Britain 1981 (paperbound)
Second impression 1981

Printed in Italy for Hodder Dargaud Ltd,
Mill Road, Dunton Green, Sevenoaks, Kent
by F.lli Pagano S.p.A. — Genoa, Campomorone

All rights reserved. No part of this publication may be
reproduced or transmitted in any form or by any means,
electronic, or mechanical, including photocopy, recording,
or any information storage and retrieval system, without
permission in writing from the publisher.

We are passing through a vast and beautiful forest, the silence broken only by the twittering of birds . . . so begins the film of *The Twelve Tasks of Asterix.* And so begins this book (minus the birdsong!). The year is 50 BC and Gaul is entirely occupied by the Romans . . . entirely? No! Somewhere in Armorica, one small village of indomitable Gauls is still holding out against the invaders . . .

AND NOW FOR THE STORY OF THE FILM.

Here we have a family group, showing the inhabitants of that little village which dared to resist the Romans. The gentleman perched on the shield is the formidable Vitalstatistix, undisputed chief of the village. His wife answers to the name of Impedimenta (Pedimenta for short), and formidable though Vitalstatistix may be, she has an irritating way of borrowing his shield and his shield-bearers when she wants to go shopping. To the extreme right, you can see the bard Cacofonix. There is some difference of opinion among the bard's contemporaries as to his musical gifts; perhaps he is just a little in advance of his time.

On his left stands his chief critic, the village blacksmith, Fulliautomatix, whose subtle method of expressing disapproval is to hammer Cacofonix into the ground. The little dog in front of the group is Dogmatix, the village mascot, and a great friend of Obelix, the menhir delivery-man. To be perfectly honest, we have to admit there are only two really sensible people in the village: Getafix, the druid with the long white beard, and the famous warrior Asterix. In fact it is thanks to these two, and Getafix's magic potion, that the Gaulish village has managed to hold out against the Romans up till now.

This magic potion gives to anyone who drinks it superhuman strength . . . for a limited period. From time to time Getafix prescribes it for his fellow villagers, all except Obelix, who fell into the cauldron as a baby, and the potion had a permanent effect on him. Poor Obelix is furious at being left out, since he hates to miss the chance of tasting anything that smells as good as the magic potion.

And now the introductions are over . . . and here comes a column of Roman legionaries advancing towards the village. Even the least observant among you may notice that the attackers do not seem exactly eager for the fray . . .

Below, we have a scene typical of Armorica at this period. Obelix, delighted at the prospect of a fight, is hurling himself upon the Romans with shouts of 'Leave them to me!' He is followed by Asterix, Vitalstatistix, and the rest of the villagers, all ready and willing to thump the enemy. The battle, as usual, is short and sharp, and in the bottom picture you see the final result: weapons twisted out of shape, and Romans tastefully scattered around the battlefield. If we come closer, they can be heard exchanging bitter comments such as:

'Another defeat! Told you so!'

'Those Gauls just aren't human!'

'You've got a point. Ordinary mortals could never resist the might of the Roman army! They must be gods!'

'And it's a fat lot of use fighting gods!'

'Tell you what . . . I'm going to Rome to tell Caesar!'

No sooner said than done. Collecting his belongings, the centurion sets off for Rome, where he meets Julius Caesar himself. Like the good soldier he is, pluck to the backbone, he makes his report. It cannot be said that this raises the Roman dictator's spirits to heights of delirious joy. The fact is, Caesar is fed to the back teeth with the little Gaulish village, its inhabitants and their magic potion. He summons his chief counsellors immediately.

The first counsellor sums up the situation very neatly: 'Suppose they really are gods, O Caesar, we're in a bit of a fix. Take an example . . . the demi-god Hercules. Anyone fancy a fight with Hercules?'

However, Caesar fails to appreciate this accurate definition of the problem, and starts roaring, 'I, Caesar, will show you that those half-wit Gauls are mere mortals! I shall go and see them! I shall set them certain tasks which only gods could perform . . . if they really are gods, and they perform my tasks successfully, I'll admit defeat. But if they are only men, they will feel the full force of Caesar's anger!'

And soon afterwards (as we usually say in the *Asterix* books, though in this case, taking into account the transport of the time, it must have been about a month later) we meet Caesar once again, engaged in conversation with Vitalstatistix outside the village gates. Thanks to a tape recorder cunningly concealed in an amphora, we have been able to preserve the gist of this historic conversation, which was to lead to the most famous bet ever made in the ancient world.

Caesar: I have come to make you a proposition, O Gauls! Your defiance of me is bad for my reputation. Back in Rome, people are beginning to laugh at me! Some of them say you must be gods. If that's so, it would explain your superhuman strength; it's no use trying to fight gods. So if you can prove that you're gods, I will admit defeat and lay down my arms.

Vitalstatistix: And just how do you want me and my mates to prove we're gods, Julius?

Caesar: Ever heard of Hercules?

Vitalstatistix: Hercules Plus, the amphora seller?

Caesar: No, no! Hercules the demigod! He performed twelve tasks so successfully that the gods recognized him as one of themselves and admitted him to Olympus . . .

Vitalstatistix: What tasks?

To help him answer this question, Caesar produces a piece of parchment (reproduced here, below left) and sets about improving Vitalstatistix's classical education.

Caesar: Hercules . . . yes, Hercules strangled the Nemean lion; killed the Lernean hydra; caught the Erymanthian boar alive; hunted down the stag with the brazen feet; shot the Stymphalian birds; tamed the bull sent by Neptune to plague Minos, king of Crete; killed Diomedes, king of Thrace; conquered the Amazons; cleansed the Augean stables; killed Geryon; stole the golden apples from the Garden of the Hesperides; and freed Theseus from the underworld . . .

Obelix, who has kept his mouth shut so far, now asks, 'Right, so what's the second task?'

While Caesar is recovering, Vitalstatistix gets his own question in. 'You mean you want us to do all these daft things, just to prove we're gods?'

Caesar: Not exactly . . . all that's a bit out of date now. With the help of my counsellors, I have drawn up a new set of tasks for you . . . if you refuse to try them, it proves you're only a bunch of crazy half-wits!

Stung to the quick ('We are *not* a bunch of half-wits!') the Gauls agree to accept Caesar's challenge. Caesar introduces them to Caius Tiddlus, who is to act as referee.

Rome, our friends assemble in the chief's hut to discuss things.

Vitalstatistix, who has had time to cast his eye over the list of tasks, has lost some of his enthusiasm.

'Hmm . . . old Julius has really got it in for us! Look at these tasks!'

'I'm always telling you!' interrupts Getafix. 'You get so carried away, and you don't stop to think till later . . .'

'Still, we couldn't let him call us a bunch of half-wits, could we?'

'Well, no . . . no, Obelix . . . however . . .'

At this point, proving himself a true leader of men, Vitalstatistix makes the necessary decision:

'Asterix, you're the cleverest of us, and Obelix is the strongest. You're the two most likely to succeed. We'll all meet in Rome to accept Caesar's surrender!'

Getafix the druid, still rather worried by his friends' enthusiasm and optimism, hands Asterix a gourd full of magic potion.

Now comes the moving scene, manly and affecting at the same time, in which we see the two heroes leave the village, to the cheers of the people. However, Obelix seems to have something on his mind . . . he is looking for a face in the crowd.

Obelix: Notice anything, Asterix?
Asterix: Notice what?
Obelix: Don't you think it's funny Cacofonix hasn't turned up to give us a farewell song?

When the summit conference has ended with a dignified Roman 'Ave!' and an informal Gaulish 'So long!', and Julius Caesar has started back to

In fact, Cacofonix had every intention of singing in honour of our heroes' departure, but unfortunately an extremely powerful fist came between this idea and its execution. At this point in our story, we must ask you to imagine the picture (one of the lost treasures of antiquity) of the bard, his lyre around his neck, being hammered into the ground by a fellow villager with a chronic aversion to the beauties of Gaulish folksong . . .

. But here comes Caius Tiddlus, in his usual sprightly manner. He unrolls the scroll bearing the list of tasks. 'Right, now for the first task!' he says, in a faint voice. 'Follow me, please.' Then he leads our friends towards the forest.

Here we meet a curious character, obviously a Greek, crouched motionless in the posture of a sprinter on his starting-blocks, ready to take off. 'This is Asbestos, just back from Marathon,' explains Tiddlus. 'He beat all comers at the Olympic Games. He can run faster than a horse, faster than the storm wind howling through the trees. One of you has to beat him in a race.'

'You do it, Asterix. You're faster than me,' admits Obelix, with admirable objectivity. 'You're faster than the hoarse wind howling through the trees . . .'

FIRST TASK.

And with these stirring words, Obelix and Tiddlus walk off. 'We'll be waiting for you the other side of the forest, on the finishing line. You start when all the sand has run out of this hourglass.'

Asterix is left alone with Asbestos, the marathon runner, still motionless on his marks. As he waits for the sand to run out of the hourglass and give the signal to start, Asterix tries to strike up a conversation with his opponent.

'Fancy that . . . a real Olympic champion! Very interesting. You know, we have athletics in our village too, but of course it isn't very exciting because we all have magic potion to drink . . . hey, are you listening to me? You aren't? Oh, well . . . I was saying it's not very exciting because we all finish at the same time, so we have to draw lots for the winner. You notice that I don't need any magic potion before a race; I've always been a very fast runner and I . . . Hey! Where are you going? Wait for me, can't you?'

Abestos pays no attention whatever. The sand has all run out, and he has started running. He is a real streak of lightning! The birds who watch him pass by get their feathers ruffled.

At this point Asterix produces his gourd of magic potion and takes a swig . . .

... the results of which may be seen on this page, centre left. They might be described as impressive. Asbestos is impressed, for one. Flying through the air like a bullet, he is much surprised when he suddenly hears Asterix saying, 'Not a bad start, old fellow! You nearly took me by surprise! The fact is, I forgot to watch the hourglass while we were chatting, and ...'

At this, Asbestos puts on a spurt. A couple of detonations ring out ... Asbestos has broken the sound barrier! As for Asterix ... well, Asterix disappears for a moment, and then we see him abreast of Asbestos again. By this time Asbestos has completely lost his cool. 'I got a bit held up back there,' says

Asterix, apologetically. 'I stopped to pick some mushrooms ... I like picking flowers too ...'

At about this moment a resounding crash is heard. Asbestos has just collided with a tree. His nose swells up enormously. On the other side of the forest, Tiddlus is waving a flag, and Asterix, holding Asbestos by the hand like the gentleman he is, crosses the finishing line first ... the winner!

'Funny thing,' says Obelix, 'he seems to have improved his Grecian profile! He has a nice Gaulish nose now ...'

Phlegmatic as ever, Tiddlus makes a mark on the list of tasks: 'First task successfully performed! Next ...'

YOUR SECOND TASK IS TO THROW THE JAVELIN FARTHER THAN VERSES THE PERSIAN.

Leaving Asbestos (who is now being overtaken by a tortoise), Tiddlus, Asterix and Obelix meet a man waiting for them in the middle of a large plain. He is a curious-looking person. He wears a pointed cap and sports a curly beard, but his most striking feature is the development of his right arm and shoulder, which are much, much larger than his left arm and shoulder. Two javelins are planted in the ground beside him. Tiddlus performs the introductions in his polite, precise and neutral voice. 'This is Verses the Persian, the most amazing javelin thrower the world has ever known. Your second task is to throw the javelin farther than Verses.'

Without sparing our friends a glance, Verses picks up one of the javelins at a sign from Tiddlus. Obelix can hardly tear his eyes away from their opponent's right arm and shoulder. 'Hey, Asterix, do you think that arm and shoulder look good? Personally, I wouldn't fancy it. I think it looks better to be nicely covered all over, like me . . . more symmetrical . . . '

While Obelix is talking, Verses has been taking his run-up, and he throws the javelin with amazing force. Asterix and Obelix do their best to follow its flight, but it disappears into the heavens at tremendous speed. Verses, very pleased with himself, roars with laughter.

Up above, the javelin speeds on its way, over lands and seas as yet undiscovered before it starts to slow down. And here it is, coming to earth. Sad to relate, there is someone underneath. A strange someone, too, his head covered with feathers, taking a nap outside his house. With a piercing whistle, the javelin lands right in front of him. Instantly, the strange person leaps up, waving a hatchet and shouting, 'War! Our enemies have declared war!' (To be perfectly accurate, the hatchet is a tomahawk, the house is a tipi and the strange person himself is a Red Indian, but Christopher Columbus will be coming along later to explain all that.)

Verses the Persian, sure he has won, is just offering our friends the second javelin.

'Let me have a go, Asterix!'

'All right, Obelix. But mind you throw it as hard as you can!'

'Just you watch!'

Obelix has seized the javelin, and under the scornful eyes of Verses, who thinks poorly of the length of his run-up, he throws it. A second or so later the javelin disappears into the clouds. Asterix, Obelix and Verses stand there trying to watch its flight. Suddenly Asterix turns round, shouting, 'Watch out!' Verses turns too . . . and lets out a great yell of terror. Obelix's throw has sent the javelin all the way round the world, and here it comes back again, making straight for Verses. Verses starts to run, but though Obelix seemed to be putting so little effort into it he threw the javelin with such force that Verses has to run a long, long time to get away. A very long time indeed . . . so long that he and the javelin end up in the camp where the Indians, much upset by the arrival of the first javelin, are in the middle of a fierce fight. They stop fighting for a moment to watch Verses pass, still with the javelin after him. Meanwhile, Tiddlus is leading our friends on again.

16

We now find our friends inside a great stadium. Pointing out a pair of massive gates at one end, Tiddlus explains, 'Now you are going to face Cylindric the German. He will come in through those gates.'

'See the size of them, Obelix? This Cylindric the German must be big!'

'Huh! I like them best big . . . big and strong!'

A gong sounds, the two enormous gates begin to open . . . tension is mounting! And into the arena walks a jolly little man wearing a judo outfit, with a black belt round his neat little paunch.

'Is *that* Cylindric the German?' exclaims Asterix.

'Leave him to me, Asterix! I'll finish him off quickly, and then we can go on to the next task.'

'All right, but watch out . . . there must be a catch in it somewhere. Those are funny clothes . he's wearing . . .'

'Oh, the robe doesn't make the Druid! Watch this!'

And Obelix marches with determination towards the mat in the centre of the stadium. The cheerful little German bows to him.

'Ach . . . zer fat chentleman first.'

'I AM NOT FAT!'

Obelix lunges furiously. With a single movement, the German takes his arm and lifts him into the air. Then, without letting go, and swinging Obelix's huge body in the air above his head, he beats the mat with him.

Asterix comes up and starts talking to Cylindric, who is still thumping Obelix up and down on the mat with gusto.

Asterix (admiringly): I say, what a splendid way to fight! I've never seen anything like it.

Cylindric (pleased, but modest): Ach, ja! I haf it vhen on my travels learnt. Long, long travels, far away. You like to haf a go, ja?

Asterix (eagerly): Oo, yes!

The German finishes wiping the floor with Obelix, stands facing Asterix, and starts the lesson:

'Is easy! You haf only to use zer man's own strength to get him down! Zer stronger he is, zer better for you.'

'Easy . . . you're only saying that because you're so strong!'

'Nein, nein! Vord of honour! Try! Here, you take mine hand . . . you put your foot zere . . . gif a heave backwards . . .'

Cylindric moves towards Asteri who grabs the German's arm a starts wiping the floor with him in h turn.

'Like this?'

'Ja! Ja! Ver' gut! You get ze ide Harder! Faster!' And Asterix, willing pupil, does as he is told, befo the dazed eyes of Obelix, who watching the scene with interes though still in a state of son confusion.

t! Zer next ding, vhen you haf me
vn on zer ground, you take
antage zat I am giddy and so you
up on me! Ja! Gut! Ver', ver' gut!
    Now you jump me on zer
mach!'
Like this?'
Ja! Gut! You take hold mine arm,
zis, zen you pull . . . now zer legs
 . . . wunderbar! And so you see, I
't move at all . . . vhy, you
 . . .'

Here Cylindric the German stops
short. He is not half so cheerful now!
He has just realized that Asterix has
tricked him; his voice dies away as he
finishes, 'You haf . . . you haf beaten
me!'

At the same moment, up in the
spectators' seats, the imperturbable
Tiddlus crosses another task off his
list.

In Rome, however, the atmosphere
is stormy, for Caesar has just heard

the results of the first tests.

'Not that it proves anything.
They've not had much to cope with so
far, but now . . . now . . . they will
have to tackle the priestesses of the
Isle of Pleasure!'

And we had better move out of
range, for at this point Caesar bursts
into fearsome, hysterical laughter.
Nor are we the only ones to retreat
instinctively; look at the poor counsellors at the far end of the table!

With Caesar's laughter still ringing in our ears, we rejoin Asterix, Obelix and Tiddlus on the banks of a lake with a little island in the middle of it. Pointing to the water, Tiddlus explains, 'You have to cross this lake. I'll wait for you on the other side. But in my opinion – and this is the first time I've offered it – you'll never make it across that lake! There's a boat over there. Well, goodbye.'

And off goes Tiddlus, leaving our two friends alone. They soon get on board the boat and start to row.

'Hey, Asterix, this task is dead easy! We'll reach the other side in no time!'

'We'd better be careful, though, Obelix . . . you never can tell.'

And here a melodious and tuneful song interrupts the two Gauls. The singing comes from the little island in the middle of the lake. By common and unspoken consent, and rowing with a precision that would do credit to a Boat Race crew, our two friends put on an incredible turn of speed. When they land (very noisily) they are welcomed by a group of beautiful young girls. The island itself is enchanting: there are flowers every- where, animals making music, and butterflies flitting about in time to the

tunes. One of the girls, in that dulcet voice adopted at a later date by the ladies at the information desks of airports, addresses the Gauls. 'Welcome to the Isle of Pleasure . . . the island you will never leave! You will stay here for ever. We were expecting you . . . kindly come this way . . .'

And now an unforgettable experi- ence begins for Asterix and Obelix. While some of the young ladies scatter

flowers over them, others dance fo their entertainment (they do a ver good samba!) while others again pou them drinks. It is like Paradise (sorry Olympus!). At a certain moment, on of the girls – she happens to be th Chief Priestess – comes up to Obelix all tender, loving affection. Givin him a kiss, she asks, 'And now, bol warrior, what would you like?'

'A boar to eat,' says Obeli hopefully.

'You're here on the Isle of Pleasure, the Chief Priestess asks you what you'd like . . . and you ask for food?'

'Why not? Eating's a pleasure, isn't it?'

'All right,' she snaps. 'We can offer nectar and ambrosia.'

'Nectar and . . . ? No fear! None of that boring old stuff! I want a nice wild boar!'

'But there aren't any boars on this island!'

'What . . . no boars, and you expect me to stay on this island of yours for ever? I ask you! That's a bit much, it really is!'

Naturally, the other girls join in the conversation, voices rising stridently . . .

'Push off, fatty! You think I'd lower myself to do your cooking?'

'Why not the washing-up too?'

'And the housework?'

'And fetch your slippers?'

The mere recital of all these horrors is too much for the Chief Priestess. Pointing to the lake, she yells, 'Push off! Get out!'

No further invitation is needed. Obelix marches furiously off towards the bank. 'You bet your life I'm pushing off, by Toutatis! Not a wild boar in sight, and they have the nerve to call this the Isle of Pleasure! Huh!'

But Asterix, his nose buried in a flower and his eyes riveted to a vision of well-rounded delight, has not heard a word of Obelix's outburst.

As he passes Asterix, Obelix shouts, 'Come on, Asterix! Get a move on! This is a rotten café!' And he dives into the lake.

Asterix, who somehow does not seem quite his usual self, turns towards the spot where Obelix has just disappeared. He takes a faltering step that way, but the Chief Priestess, recovering her nice manners and her dulcet voice, sidles up to him, cooing invitingly, 'Let him go . . . stay with us! We will give you pleasure such as the gods themselves enjoy . . . '

By now the suspense is killing us! Will Asterix succumb? We are all holding our breath . . . until a loud and very cross voice is heard. 'Asterix!' It is Obelix. And Asterix, awakened from his dream at last, jumps into the lake too. He must be in a rather curious condition, since as he enters the water it hisses and a cloud of steam rises, as if something very hot had been plunged into it.

After a pleasantly refreshing little swim, we find our friends back with Tiddlus, who crosses out yet another task on the list with his stylus. Then he jerks his thumb at a little temple built in the Egyptian style.

'And now you have to look deep into the dreadful eyes of Iris, the great Egyptian magician . . . '

Obelix, a little worried, notices something odd. 'See that, Asterix? He was flying low. That means we'll have rain, and . . . ' But the harsh voice of Iris calls, 'Next, please!' It is the Gauls' turn now. Seeing them come in, Iris raises his eyes. 'What's all this? Oh yes, I remember now . . . two Gauls. I was expecting you! You . . . the little one . . . sit there, please.' And Iris makes Asterix sit opposite him. His eyes light up like a couple of light-houses. They are dazzling. 'By Osiris and by Apis, look at me . . . '

But Asterix interrupts. Much impressed, he inquires, 'I say, how do you do that with your eyes?'

'Shut up, Gaul!'

Our two friends enter the temple, to find themselves in a large hall which is obviously a waiting room. A little man is already sitting there, reading magazines. From the room next door comes an impressive voice: 'By Osiris and by Apis, look at me, look into my eyes . . . You have turned into a cat . . . yes, a cat!' There is a brief silence, the door opens, and out comes a curious character on all fours. Before leaving the temple he rubs against the legs of the little man who is waiting, and mews.

'Next, please!'

The little man gets up and goes into the magician's room.

Soon we hear the voice of Iris again. 'By Osiris and by Apis, look into my eyes! By Osiris and by Apis, you have turned into a bird . . . yes, a bird!'

Again there is a sinister little silence, then the door slowly opens and the little man comes out, fluttering around the room. Then he takes off in a long, soaring flight . . .

Iris's voice is terrible, his eyes are a dreadful sight, but Asterix, like any good Gaul, wants to know how the trick is done. He persists. 'Can you light them up one at a time?'

'Silence! I'm concentrating! Er . . . where was I? Oh yes! By Osiris and by Apis, you have turned into a boar . . .'

'It must be useful for reading in bed.'

'You are . . . you are . . .'

'I'm a boar . . .'

'That's it! I'm a boar! By Opis and Asiris, I'm a boar . . .! And so on . . . until the moment when Iris, unable to bear it, dashes out of the temple, grunting ferociously . . .

'Alors, you are expected, monsieur! I bring in ze banquet right away!' As Obelix sits down and tucks a napkin under his chin, Calorifix disappears into the kitchens. He is soon back, carrying an enormous roast boar surrounded by chips. 'What's this?' asks Obelix, pointing to a chip. 'Ah, zees I 'ave invent myself. Ees shape like ze cheeps of wood, but grow in ze ground. I 'ave not yet found ze good name, but I think it be ze big success, no?'

Obelix gets to work on the boar, which is soon looking pretty silly. Never mind, Calorifix is back already with another dish . . .

There is a swing-door into the kitchen, and every time it swings open Calorifix comes back with more to

Leaving Iris, who now thinks he is a boar, to his own devices, along with the man who thinks he is a cat and the man who thinks he is a bird, Asterix and Obelix rejoin Tiddlus, who leads them to an inn. 'Your next task will be to eat every morsel of the meal prepared for you by Calorifix, the

great chef of the Titans. No mortal man has ever been able to get through one of his enormous meals, but you will have to eat it all, down to the very last crumb. Enjoy yourselves!'

'An interesting kind of task at last . . . !' Yes, quite right: that was Obelix, marching into the inn, rubbing his hands. He is welcomed by the famous chef Calorifix, in his interesting foreign accent.

eat. He praises his creations in lyrica terms. 'Ze ox! Ees good, ze ox! Z geese! Geese ees good, zey are fat! Z nice flock of muttons . . . I 'ope yo like. Ze 'ole school of fish! Ze cow an ze veals . . . ees not right to separat ze family! Ze great Titanic ome lette . . . eight dozen eggs! Ze came Zis you will like. Eet 'ave ze goo stuffing too.' And so the banquet goe on, to the sound of an impressiv musical backing (jawbones *allegro prestissimo*) kindly provided by Obelix.

Meanwhile, it is getting dark outside, but Asterix does not seem to be worried . . . and in the end Calorifix stumbles out of the inn door, very upset indeed. 'Did he eat the lot?' asks Tiddlus. This is just too much for the unhappy chef, who bursts into tears. 'Yes! Yes! I 'ave nozzing left in ze kitchen. Nozzing!' As Calorifix disappears, Obelix emerges . . . a slightly disappointed Obelix, asking, 'Did anyone see which way that chef went? He let me down when I'd only had a few starters!'

Leaving Calorifix to nurse his sorrows, our friends and Tiddlus now make for a cave in the mountainside.

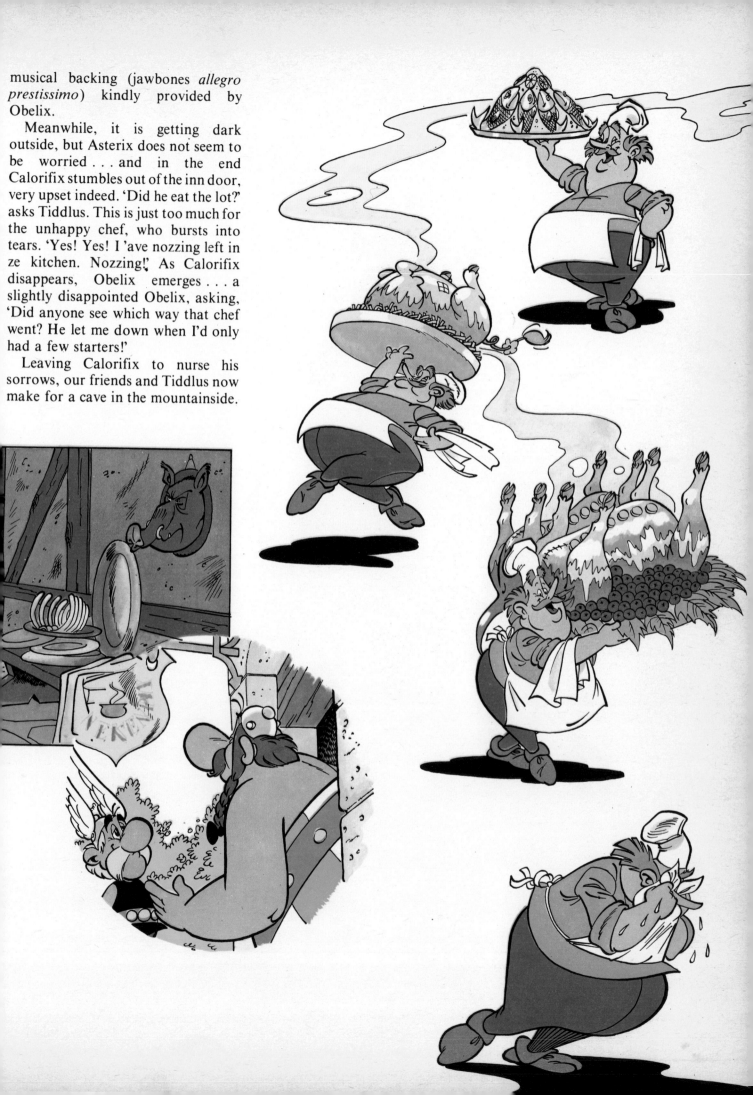

Soon they find themselves at the cave entrance. It is shaped like a monstrous mouth, and Tiddlus explains their next task. 'You must go into the Cave of the Beast.'

'Beast? What Beast?' asks Asterix. 'And what is this Beast like?'

'I've no idea. No one has ever come out alive . . .' And with these words, Tiddlus leaves them.

Inside the cave it is pitch dark, but noisy. We hear sinister laughter, and the screeching of horrible birds flying low as they pass. This reminds Obelix of something. 'Hey, Asterix . . .'

'Yes, I know; they're flying low, we shall have rain.'

'Well, if they think they can frighten us they're wrong, because everyone knows we fear only one thing, the sky falling on our heads, and . . .'

'Watch out, Obelix!' For, with a terrifying roar, a nightmare device has nearly run our two friends down.

'What was that, Asterix?'

'I've no idea, but I'm beginning to get fed up. I wonder what the time is . . .'

'Twelve noon. I could do with feeding up too.'

'Don't say you feel hungry again!'

'I always feel hungry at twelve noon! I could eat anything . . . anything at all!' And at these forceful words a tremendous row breaks out, followed by a very confused free-for-all . . . we next find Asterix and Obelix emerging through the manhole cover of the Cave of the Beast, and back with Tiddlus again on the terrace of an inn.

'Forgive my curiosity, but what *was* the Beast like?' asks Tiddlus.

'Very tasty!' replies Obelix happily, giving the waiter his order. 'I'd like a drink to wash it down!'

The inn where our friends are sitting looks out on a street full of very peculiar characters. All the passers-by seem very agitated. We hear raucous laughter, we see eyes swivelling round and round, we see people walking on their hands. A woman comes running past, waving her arms about and clucking like a frightened hen. She is pursued by a suspicious-looking character brandishing an enormous hatchet and licking his lips. The couple pass a personage of obvious importance, having a bath in a tub carried by four slaves, but they take no notice of him. Finally, despite his equable nature, Asterix can no longer conceal his surprise.

'Oh,' says Tiddlus, 'these people have all been in the place that sends you mad.'

'Place that sends you mad?'

'Yes, and you have to go there too; that's your next task.' And Tiddlus points out a vast building nearby.

'What do we have to do in there?'

'Nothing much. You have to get hold of a certain permit which allows you to go on to the next task.'

'I see. Just a simple administrative formality?'

'That's right . . . an administrative formality. Ask for Permit A38.'

'Well, off we go, Obelix.'

No sooner said than done. Our friends enter the building.

'What is it?' the desk clerk asks, ungraciously.

'We want a Permit Number A38.'

The desk clerk cups his hand around his ear. 'Want to register a galley? They've sent you to the wrong place. You want the harbourmaster's office, down by the port.'

'What?' And realizing, like ourselves, that the desk clerk is deaf as a post, Asterix goes on patiently, 'No. We do not want to register a galley. We want Permit Number A38.'

'The port? It's the other end of town, by the seaside, you can't miss it . . .'

'But we don't want to go to the port! We want Permit A38!'

'What?'

'PERMIT A38!'

'There's no need to shout! What manners! Where do you think you are, by Jupiter? Apply at Window number one, left-hand corridor, last door on the right.'

Our friends follow his instructions, only to find that there is no door at all on the right in the left-hand corridor. 'Let's try the door opposite,' suggests Asterix. They walk into a small, bare room. A large civil servant is sitting on a swing in the middle of the room, while a pretty girl pushes him. At the sight of his visitors, the civil servant stops swinging. He is furious.

'Who said you could come in?'

'Er . . . we want Window one.'

'Then consult the floor plan up on the sixth floor . . . !'

On the sixth floor, they find that the proper place to go is Window two. Here two clerical workers are engaged in animated conversation. 'You know *her* . . . and mind you, she can't even afford to keep a slave . . .'

'Please, miss . . .' (Asterix, trying to attract the lady's attention.)

'She sold off her Iberian, claiming she preferred to do her own housework, but . . .'

'Please, miss!' (Asterix again. He is getting annoyed.)

'Can't you see I'm busy? Now, where was I? Oh, yes! Poor old Claudius! You know, he . . .'

'PLEASE, MISS!' (Asterix's irritation is increasing visibly.)

'Oh, by Jupiter! How rude people are these days! Well, what do you want?'

'Permit A38.'

'Have you filled in the blue form?'

'Blue form? No.'

'Then how do you think you're going to get Permit A38?'

'So where do I get the blue form?'

'Window one. Now, where was I . . . ?'.

And it is the same story as the Gauls make their way all round the building . . .

'The blue form? No, not here. Try Window seven, fifth floor . . .'

'The green form . . . Window fourteen . . .'

Mingling with the babble of voices, we hear such remarks as: 'I told you, the port is by the seaside!' 'Can't you see I'm busy?' and finally a voice roars out, 'STOP IT!' Obelix's nerves have cracked up under the strain. 'Asterix, we'll never get out of here . . . the magic potion won't be any use in this place! We shall go mad, and end up as Caesar's slaves!'

'Not if I know it. I have an idea! We'll fight them with their own weapons. Watch this!'

And Asterix starts going round asking for Permit Number A39 'as stipulated in the new circular B65', which of course exists only in his own fertile imagination. The trick comes off! Soon the building is in a state of ferment, as everyone searches for this mysterious new document. The tumult is at its height in the entrance hall, where only the Prefect seems to be keeping his cool. Seeing this, Asterix decides to strike while the iron is hot. 'Please, sir . . .'

'I'm very busy just now! What do you want?'

'Permit A38!'

The Prefect produces a small slab from the folds of his toga and, in some annoyance, hands it to Asterix. 'Here you are! Now kindly get out. Some people here are trying to work!'

And as Asterix and Obelix leave the building, we hear the Prefect give a great peal of demented laughter.

With these words, Tiddlus informs
our friends of the nature of their next
task. Obelix has a bright idea. 'Why
don't we cross the abyss down below,
instead of walking over the wire? I can
see a little river, but the water looks
calm . . .'

'Ah, yes, but in fact that little river is
full of crocodiles . . . very sacred
crocodiles, given to Caesar by Queen
Cleopatra of Egypt. And they are
very, very savage!'

'Yuk! I don't like crocodiles. I tried
them once . . . they were stringy.
Come on, Asterix!'

Asterix complies, and the two of
them set off across the abyss. But it is
not easy to master tightrope walking
at the first attempt!

They proceed, contorting their bodies, arms outstretched; the wire sags beneath them, and our friends indulge in all sorts of acrobatics before they finally fall. Asterix grabs hold of the wire and Obelix grabs hold of Asterix's legs. They stay like that for a moment; then we hear a deep sigh and see them glance into space.

'Oh, well,' says Obelix, 'I suppose we'll have to. Coming, Asterix?'

'Wait a moment . . . ' Asterix lets go of the wire with one hand, takes out his gourd of magic potion and has a swig. Thunder and lightning . . .

'Here goes!' He lets go with his other hand, and they both fall. It is a long, long time before we hear two splashes as our friends hit the water. Next we hear sounds of fighting, fearsome grunts, the wild churning of the water, and above all the noise, Obelix's voice shouting, 'Filthy creatures! Nasty inedible things!' Then we see the crocodiles rising from below, looking absolutely dazed, and flying off in all directions. Reliable witnesses claim to have seen suitcases, wallets and shoes, all labelled 'Genuine Crocodile', going the same way, and there must be some truth in this story . . . at least, something particularly nasty must be going on down in the abyss, since the crocodiles prefer to stay clinging to the wire rather than go down again.

All the two Gauls have to do now is
rejoin Tiddlus, who has been fishing
as he waits for them on the edge of the
abyss.

'And now you must climb the
highest mountain in these parts. At
the top you will find the Old Man of
the Mountains, who will ask you a
riddle.'

'Couldn't this old man come down
here to ask us his riddle?'

'Come on, Obelix, don't be lazy! Off
we go!'

And our friends start climbing. The
going gets harder and harder, until the
rockface is almost vertical. There is
wind and snow. Eagles fly past close to
the climbers, but Obelix just brushes
them away as if they were bothersome
insects. Finally the moment comes
when Obelix reaches up again for the
next hand-hold, and fails to find one.
'Hey, Asterix, I've run out of
mountain . . .'

They meet a man there, an old, old
man, his voice the croaking voice of
extreme age.

'I am the Old Man of the
Mountains. Have you miserable
mortals come for my riddle?'

'Yes . . . hurry up and ask it, Old
Man of the Mountains! It's not very
warm up here, by Toutatis!'

'Do you know, foolish men, that if
you fail to give the right answer you
will be plunged instantly into the
depths of Hell?'

'What, after climbing all this way?'
Obelix is indignant. 'I call that a bit
steep!'

'O presumptuous mortals . . . one of you, eyes blindfolded, must tell me which of these two piles of laundry was washed in Olympus, the divine detergent!'

Asterix volunteers for the task. A few seconds later, he points to one of the piles. 'This one!'

'Yes!' The Old Man's voice is younger, stronger! He is holding up a detergent packet. 'You got it right! You recognized Olympus! The gods themselves do their washing with Olympus, which washes whiter and leaves your hands so, so soft! O ye gods, did you hear that? This mortal gave the right answer!'

The gods have heard all right, and in the course of a short visit to Mount Olympus we discover that the way people who would like to be gods too keep getting the riddle right is beginning to annoy them a good deal . . . so much, in fact, that Jupiter lets loose a violent thunderstorm!

Meanwhile, Asterix and Obelix have gone back down to the plain at the foot of the mountain. Tiddlus tells them they will have to spend the night there. 'Good idea,' says Asterix. 'I'm rather tired.'

However, while our friends are sleeping soundly, some strange Roman legionaries appear on the scene. Obelix, woken by the noise they make, rubs his hands in glee. 'Goody! Romans, all for me!' And he makes for them. But much to his surprise, his fists meet thin air. This is too much for Obelix. The phantom legionaries roar with mocking laughter. 'Don't bother your head, poor mortal! We are ghosts . . . departed spirits who haunt this place. All who venture to spend the night here die of fear . . . ha, ha, ha!'

'What's all this row in aid of?' A furious interruption from Asterix. 'Do you know what the time is?' Obelix tries to explain that the ghosts are only trying to keep their poor departed spirits up, but Asterix is not impressed. 'We've run a big race, we've tackled priestesses, magicians, chefs, civil servants, crocodiles, and we need our beauty sleep! You can keep your spirits up, but don't keep us up! Push off!'

Asterix sounds so fierce that the poor ghosts, feeling demoralized and misunderstood, decide to go back to the underworld.

Next morning we find the two Gauls waking up, much to their surprise, in front of a vast flight of steps to a palace guarded by legionaries who are far from ghostly.

'Where are we?' asks Asterix.

'You're in Rome, outside Julius Caesar's palace. Caesar is expecting you.'

'Either there's something funny going on around here, Asterix,' says Obelix, 'or the Romans have learnt to build very fast . . . '

'Oh, what does it matter? Come on, soldier, take us to your leader!'

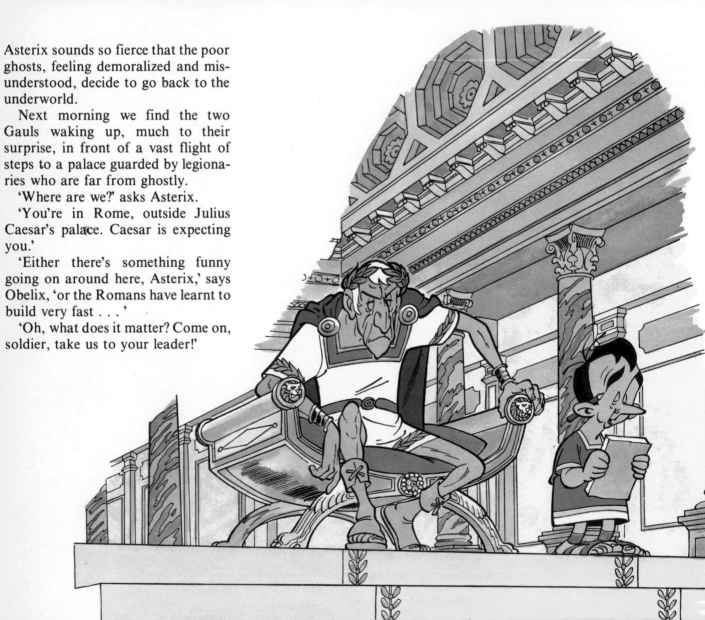

Asterix and Obelix are ushered into the presence of Caesar. Tiddlus is there too, complete with his list of tasks, his imperturbability, and his precise little voice, which announces, 'O Caesar, they have performed all the tasks, overcome every problem, and succeeded every time . . .'

'Well, Gauls, it cannot be denied that the gods have favoured you . . . but this is where your luck runs out! Your last task takes place in the Circus here in Rome, where you will be slaughtered along with all the other people from your village. They're waiting for you ther . . .'

'Oh, good! They came!'

'You will all be killed for the amusement of my people, and my triumph will be complete at last! Have you anything to add, O Gauls?'

Coming a little closer, we observe that Asterix and Obelix, always fond of a joke, cannot resist their usual comment: 'These Romans are crazy!'

We need hardly add that this gets them removed from Caesar's presence in double quick time. As the Circus Maximus begins to fill up with a happy crowd, our friends are taken off to prison, where they meet the other Gauls from their own little village. Everyone is delighted; there is a lot of shouting and laughing and hugging. Suddenly we hear thunderous applause outside. Asterix glances out at the arena through the barred window. 'Caesar has just arrived!'

Getafix, who has been over in a corner stirring something in a cauldron, announces, 'Roll up, everyone! The potion's ready!' Asterix is rightly first in the queue for a ladleful, which has its usual spectacular effect.

Meanwhile, Caesar, in his Imperial Box, is asking the Organizer of the Games, 'Well, have you carried out my instructions?'

'Yes, O Caesar. For a start, these unhappy Gauls will have to face the fiercest of our gladiators. And then if there are any survivors, we let out the wild beasts! We have lions and tigers and panthers and bears, even elephants! A lovely programme! The audience will like it!'

'All right . . . sound the trumpet the Games are about to begin!' Caesa waves his hand, and the trumpe sound. Inside the circus prison, whe everyone has now been dosed wit magic potion, the Gaulish chief Vita statistix, installed on his shield, clap his hands for silence. 'Liste everyone! The show is about to start! go in first, and you all follow me. An keep in line, please. There are going t be crowds of people there watching u so let's show a bit of dignity, right?

Obelix, however, does not entirel agree with the programme. 'And ju why do you think you should go firs O Chief Vitalstatistix?'

'Because I *am* the chief, that's why

If Vitalstatistix thought that this would clinch the argument, Obelix instantly proves him wrong. 'You may be the chief, but we've been doing all the work, haven't we, Asterix?' Asterix prefers to keep quiet, but not everyone shares his common sense and moderation . . . least of all Fulliautomatix, who now joins in, sending the ball back into Obelix's court. 'All the more reason for the rest of us to have a bit of fun now!' The argument is soon in full swing, and understandably enough Unhygienix wants to have his say too: 'That's right! Some people get all the luck!'

Witnesses of this scene who gave an account of it later all agree that it was at this point Impedimenta, the chief's wife, spoke up for chivalry and tradition. 'Nicely brought up people let women go first!'

Everyone is shouting at once.

'Women AND children first!'

'And how about me?' sings out Geriatrix.'I'm the oldest inhabitant! I've got a right to go first, haven't I?'

Meanwhile, up in the Imperial Box with the worthy Tiddlus beside him, Julius Caesar turns to the Organizer of the Games, who is waiting for his orders. 'Bring on the gladiators!'

No sooner had Julius Caesar uttered
these words than a fanfare of trumpets
echoes through the vast Circus
Maximus. The crowd sits up straight,
and silence falls (apart from a faint
sound of shouting from the Gauls'
cells). A barred gate is raised on one
side of the arena, and in march the
gladiators, striding out in single file, to
the applause of the now deliriously
enthusiastic audience. Their calm,
their strength and discipline make an
impressive sight as they stand facing
Caesar's box. At a signal, they raise
their arms and utter their famous
greeting in chorus. 'Ave Caesar!
Morituri te salutant!'

And now Caesar orders, 'Force the
Gauls into the arena!'

The trumpets sound again. Another
barred gate is slowly raised on the
other side of the arena. And
then . . . nothing! No one comes in!
More trumpets . . . rather more
insistent this time. Finally the Gauls,
still preoccupied by their own quarrel,
tumble out into the arena. They are
headed by Asterix, followed by Obelix
and Getafix; the rest of the procession
is a little less orderly. Certainly the
whole thing bears little resemblance to
the entry of condemned men into an
arena where, in theory, they are about
to die!

A heated argument is still in
progress.

'Want me to smack your great fat
face, Mister Unhygienix?'

'You just try it, Mister Obelix!'

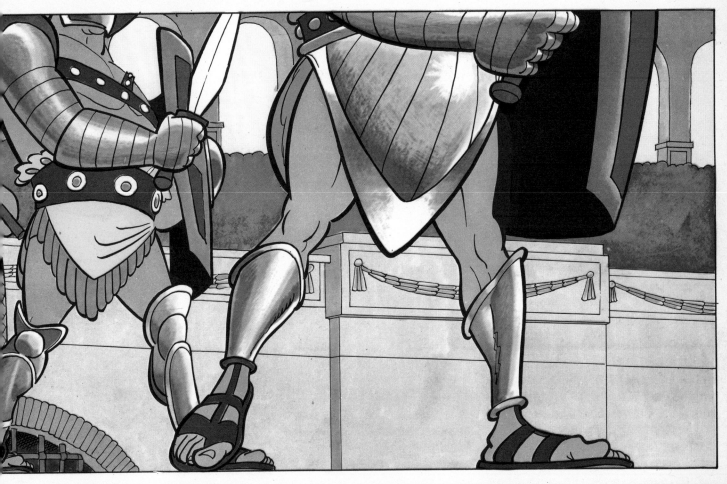

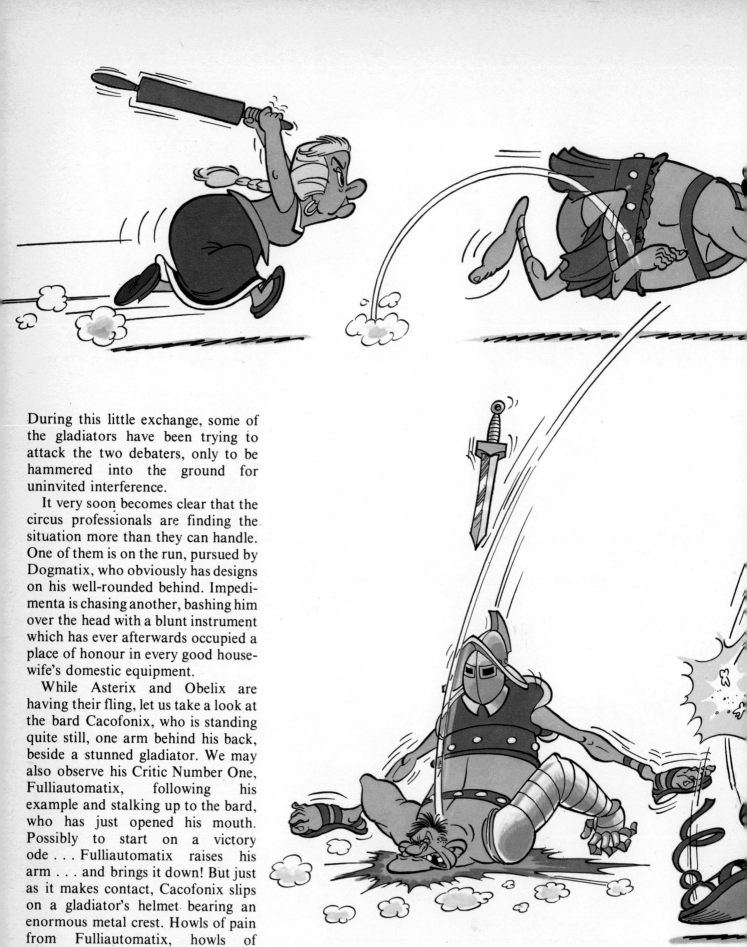

During this little exchange, some of the gladiators have been trying to attack the two debaters, only to be hammered into the ground for uninvited interference.

It very soon becomes clear that the circus professionals are finding the situation more than they can handle. One of them is on the run, pursued by Dogmatix, who obviously has designs on his well-rounded behind. Impedimenta is chasing another, bashing him over the head with a blunt instrument which has ever afterwards occupied a place of honour in every good housewife's domestic equipment.

While Asterix and Obelix are having their fling, let us take a look at the bard Cacofonix, who is standing quite still, one arm behind his back, beside a stunned gladiator. We may also observe his Critic Number One, Fulliautomatix, following his example and stalking up to the bard, who has just opened his mouth. Possibly to start on a victory ode . . . Fulliautomatix raises his arm . . . and brings it down! But just as it makes contact, Cacofonix slips on a gladiator's helmet bearing an enormous metal crest. Howls of pain from Fulliautomatix, howls of laughter from those who saw this little episode. In his box, the horror-stricken Caesar gives Tiddlus a nasty look. Tiddlus, calm as ever, is enjoying an iced lolly . . .

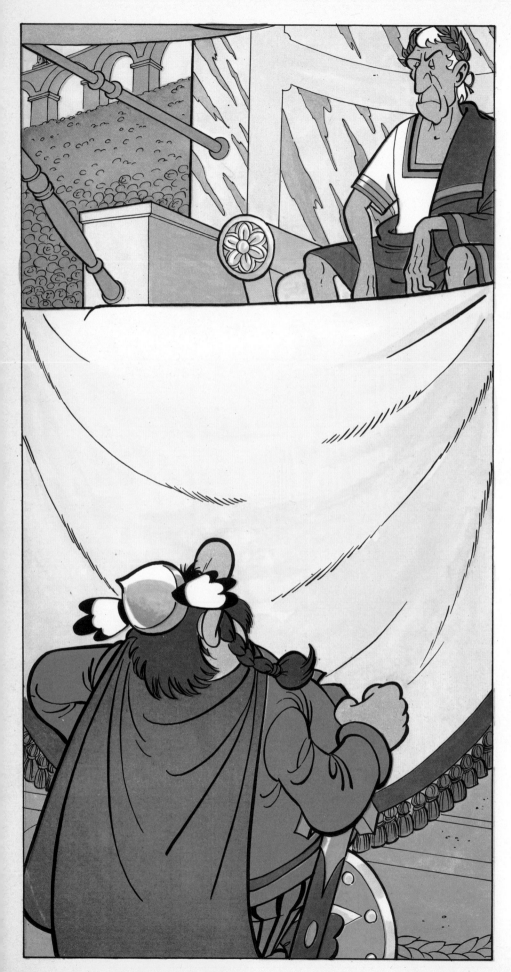

A few more thumps happily distributed about the place, and soon there is not a single able-bodied gladiator in sight. Vitalstatistix, who has had a few transport problems with his shield-bearers, now manages to have himself brought face to face with the Imperial Box. In a voice like a circus clown's, he inquires, 'O Caesar, we've finished off the gladiators! What's the next turn?'

Caesar, looking very displeased indeed, turns to the Organizer of the Games. 'Wild beasts! Bring on the wild beasts at once!' The Organizer – who looks as though he is beginning to wonder about his future career – gives a signal. The trumpets sound. But the fanfare is much less solemn this time; it sounds more like a circus tune than music suitable for an execution.

Barred gates rise all around the arena, and on come the lions, tigers, panthers, bears and elephants.

And the wild beasts go just the same way as the gladiators . . . if anything, the effect is even more striking! The animals, who may have entered the arena a little over-confidently, are brought to heel by our friends at once. A tap or so, an affectionate but firm kick here and there, and that does the trick: the animals are tamed.

Some of the Gauls bend down so that the tigers and panthers can leap gracefully over their backs. The bears dance in a dignified manner for the young (and pretty) wife of Geriatrix. In fact the wild animals, instantly grasping what the future course of history will be, spontaneously start acting like the tame circus animals we all know. The elephants do their best to form a living pyramid (Obelix has taken it into his head to organize one). Dogmatix rides grandly on a lion's back. In short, the performance is better suited to the Big Top than the sinister and blood-soaked Circus Maximus of Rome. In addition, the whole thing is accompanied by loud circus fanfares, and the applause and laughter of the audience.

The one place where no one feels in the least little bit like laughing is the Imperial Box. The Organizer of the Games is on the verge of a nervous breakdown. We hear him crying, 'They've done for the circus! The children are happy! People are laughing! It's a shame! Circuses will never be the same again!'

Caesar now turns to Tiddlus, who is holding the list of tasks. Tiddlus looks at Caesar. Then, still the perfect civil servant, imperturbable as ever, he makes one large tick on the whole thing.

And now Julius Caesar has risen to his feet. With a wave of his arm, he silences the circus. Then, in a hoarse voice, he proclaims:

'Gauls! You have performed all the twelve tasks I set you . . . so you must be gods, and it's no good trying to fight gods! You are our masters! I leave my fate and the fate of Rome in your hands.'

And Caesar takes off his laurel wreath and flings it to the ground. It falls in the sand, right at the feet of the Gauls, who have formed a smiling group in the middle of the arena. The applause is deafening. Asterix and his friends pose for the sculptor, whose souvenir group is going to puzzle historians for generations to come.

However, one question remains to be asked: what will the victorious Gauls do to the man they have overcome at the end of the twelve tasks successfully (and so stylishly!) performed by Asterix and Obelix?

We find the answer in a little Roman. villa nestling among green trees. Here is Julius Caesar, busy digging his garden and watering his flowers.

Yes . . . the magnanimous Gauls have allowed Caesar to retire to this little country villa, to live in peace and quiet, far from the burdens and cares of power . . .

'Julius! Dinner's ready!'

That was a feminine voice we heard calling Caesar . . . the voice of Cleopatra. And Caesar would no more dream of disobeying her now than before . . . in fact, less so, since he has discovered hitherto unrecognized talents in his fair companion, as witness the following remark . . .

'What a wonderful cook you are, Cleopatra dear!'

But it is time for us to leave them, if only to find out what became of the other characters in this story.

It seems a fair guess to say that Verses must still be running around the world, pursued by Obelix's javelin, Calorifix will have gone back to his ovens, the poor scared crocodiles are back in their river again, and the good Old Man of the Mountains is still plugging Olympus, the divine detergent.

As for the place that sends you mad, no doubt about that at all . . . we see evidence around us every day to prove that it went right back to functioning even more crazily than before . . .

And how about Caius Tiddlus? Calm, phlegmatic, good-natured Tiddlus, what about him? Well, he was allowed to choose his own reward for his good and faithful service. And he has decided to go into exile (!) on the Isle of Pleasure, where we see him in action, indulging every whim, his famous imperturbability gone for good.

As for our Gaulish friends, led by Asterix and Obelix, they have gone back to their quiet little village.

And all is well. Life is back to normal. Getafix the druid is still making his potions, and Cacofonix the bard has suggested 'giving them a little song' in honour of the villagers' exploits . . . a suggestion which left him, as usual, tied up at the foot of a tree.

This evening, in the little village which is now the centre of the known world, the conquerors, re-united around their chief Vitalstatistix, are getting ready to celebrate with one of their traditional banquets.

Wait a moment, though . . . what was that? I fancy I hear some of our readers raising an objection . . .

Oh . . . you were saying it doesn't seem to match up with historical fact? The Gauls never really conquered Julius Caesar? Fair enough . . . but that's the great thing about a strip cartoon, you can give your imagination full rein! What's wrong with a little wishful thinking . . . ?

'Hey, Asterix, have we real become the rulers of Rome?

'Well, let's face it, Obelix . . . lik they were saying, this is only a str cartoon. Anything goes . . .'

'Anything goes?'

And with these words Obelix disa pears from sight. Only Asterix know where he has gone . . . 'to an auste island retreat where he is getting read for our next adventures . . . but don tell anyone, it's a secret!'